My Basset Has the Sneezles

by Alex Mesias

Barbara Lieberman

Ellie Lieberman

A Pipe & Thimble Publishing Book
Lomita, CA

Other children's books by
Barbara Lieberman

The Treasure of Ravenwood

Ben's Little Acorn

Why Does The Moon Follow Me?

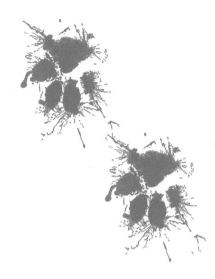

Other children's books by
Ellie Lieberman

A Dragon's Treasure

Ben's Little Tomato

The Butter Thief

My basset has the sneezles. Whatever will I do? I discovered his dilemma, when putting on my shoe.

It's bad enough
that bassets tend
to have the drools.
But now it's
combined together
With giant
snot-filled pools!

The phlegm shows
no sign of easing
and we haven't got
a clue.
I thought the drool
was bad enough, but
the snot is worse...
times two!

This was no dainty nose drip as small as morning dew,

With each projectile sneeze, Wow, the boogers really flew!

With a breeze,
then a wheeze,
I know my basset
will sneeze,
On easels and
weasles go my
basset's sneezles.

Who would've guessed all the things I bought would all be covered in juicy basset snot?

My basset has the sneezles. Whatever will I do? He snuffs and huffs and sneezes.... achoo! Achoo! ACHOO!

Despite the grossness, even with a new green upon the wall, I love him from his ears to his wrinkles, schnoz and snot and all!

Alex Mesias enjoys science fiction and fantasy. His favorite authors are Terry Pratchett and Douglas Adams. Sporting a wizard's beard, his magic extends to sewing dice bags and streaming on twitch. He enjoys video games, movies, and various tabletop/ role playing games.

Barbara Lieberman is a writer whose books are about the power of words, the power of love, and the consequences of the choices we make. A New Jersey native, Barbara moved to beautiful Southern California to start over. The proud mother of two amazing young adults, Barbara is also an avid gardener, a life-long (and long-suffering) Phillies fan, a voracious reader, and an inspirational speaker.

A New Jersey transplant, Ellie Lieberman lives now in sunny Southern California. She works with the fairies on her handmade business, Acorn Tops, when not writing or illustrating. An avid reader with a bedroom that looks like a mini library, Ellie is a lover of all things purple, basset hound, squirrel, and milk chocolate, with a slight fried rice obsession.

Made in the USA
Columbia, SC
22 February 2024

32070909R00015